Tyler Timothy Bradford and the Birthday Surprise

By Mary Lou Carney
Illustrated by Shari Warren

Columbus, Ohio

To Drake Pennington Redman,
who taught me how to be a grandmother.
–MLC

To my daughter, Alexandra Maxwell Warren,
who is also a cupcake connoisseur!
–SW

Text © 2005 Mary Lou Carney
Art © 2005 Shari Warren

Published by Gingham Dog Press, an imprint of School Specialty Children's Publishing, a member of the School Specialty Family.

Library of Congress Cataloging-in-Publication Data is on file with the publisher.

Send all inquiries to:
School Specialty Children's Publishing
8720 Orion Place
Columbus, OH 43240-2111

ISBN 0-7696-3168-1

1 2 3 4 5 6 7 8 PHXBK 09 08 07 06 05 04

Tyler Timothy Bradford started off for school when,
suddenly, he stopped and said, "There's something I forgot."

He looked at his arms.
No, it wasn't his shirt.

He looked at his feet.
No, it wasn't his shoes.

He looked in his backpack.
No, it wasn't his homework.

He looked in his lunch bag.
No, it wasn't his dessert.

Forgetting his dessert
was one thing Tyler Timothy Bradford
would *never* do, especially on days like today.
This morning, his mother had packed
ooey, gooey chocolate cupcakes
left over from his little sister's birthday party.

Birthday Party

Something deep inside Tyler Timothy Bradford seemed to wiggle at the thought of these two words. Maybe what he had forgotten had something to do with a birthday party.

"Mrs. Berry!" he yelled.

"Today is Mrs. Berry's 30th birthday!"

And then, Tyler Timothy Bradford remembered.

Every student in his class was bringing

30 of something for Mrs. Berry.

Everyone except Tyler Timothy Bradford.

Thirty. It wasn't such a terribly large number.
Maybe he had 30 of something that he could give her.

He emptied his pockets:
    1 yo-yo
    2 dimes
    1 piece of chewing gum.

He dumped his backpack onto the grass:
   1 math book
   3 pages of addition homework
   1 umbrella, in case it started to rain.
   (His mother always worried
   that it might start to rain.)

He looked in his lunch bag:
   1 tuna sandwich
   4 carrot sticks
   2 ooey, gooey chocolate cupcakes.

"Nothing even close to 30," he said.

Tyler Timothy Bradford felt terrible!
He didn't want to be the only student in his class
who didn't have a gift for Mrs. Berry!

He reached into his lunch bag and took out
an ooey, gooey chocolate cupcake.
He almost always felt better when he was
eating his mother's special cupcakes.

But this time, it didn't seem to help.
As the crumbs fell onto the sidewalk,
Tyler Timothy Bradford squatted down
and tried to think of some way to find
30 of something—and still get to school on time.

And that's when he saw them. Ants.
They trailed in a long line, heading straight for his
ooey, gooey chocolate cupcake crumbs.

"I know what I'll take her!"
Tyler Timothy Bradford said.
"It will be the best gift ever!"

Then he began walking to school, carefully dropping ooey, gooey chocolate cupcake crumbs.

When Tyler Timothy Bradford
arrived at his classroom,
Justin ran over and announced,
"I brought 30 jellybeans! What did you bring?"

"I brought 30 paper clips!" Tony said.

"I brought 30 pennies," Ally said,
dropping the shiny copper pieces
onto Mrs. Berry's desk.

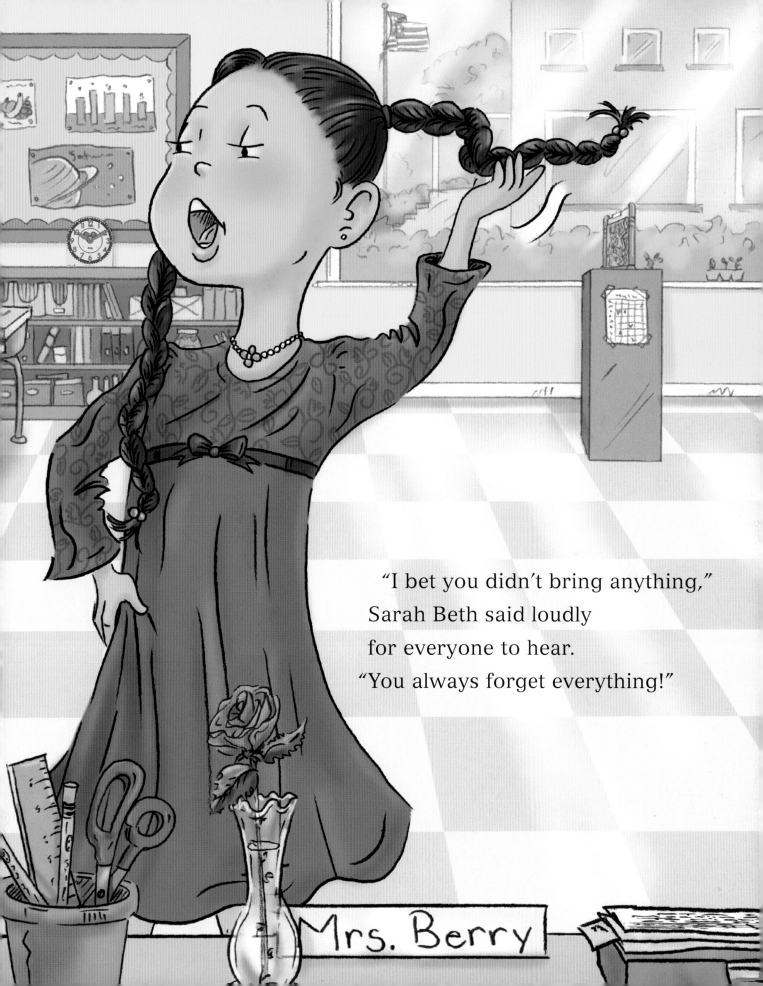

"I bet you didn't bring anything,"
Sarah Beth said loudly
for everyone to hear.
"You always forget everything!"

Mrs. Berry

But all at once,
Justin and Tony and Ally and Sarah Beth
and everyone in the room, including Mrs. Berry,
saw them.

"Ants!" Sarah Beth squealed. "He brought ants!"

A long, thin line of shiny black ants
trailed behind Tyler Timothy Bradford,
each one munching on an
ooey, gooey chocolate cupcake crumb.

For a moment, no one spoke.
Everyone could almost hear the ants
marching across the classroom floor.
Marching and marching right into the
empty ant farm at the back of the room.
They made their way, one by one,
down into the soft, rich soil
inside the big glass case.

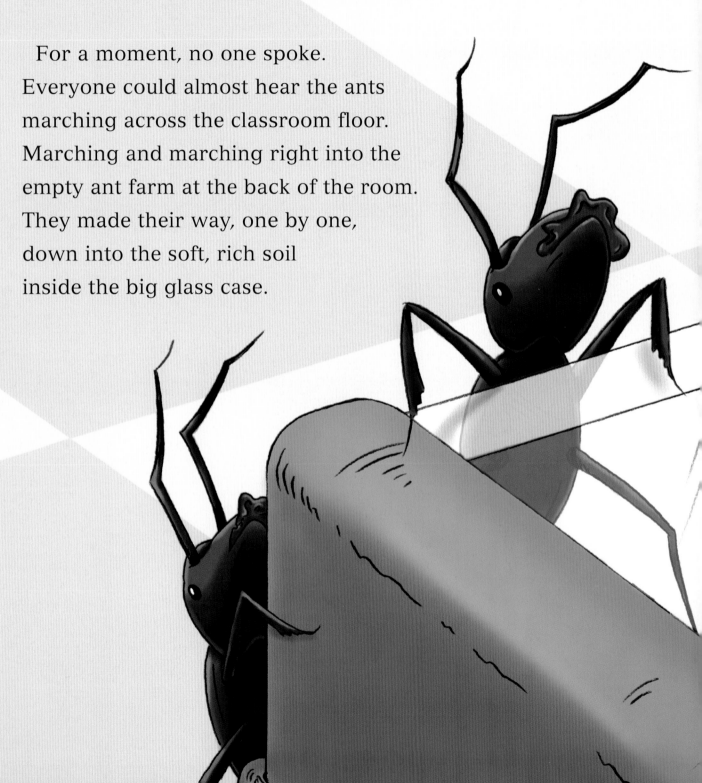

"Oh, Tyler Timothy!" exclaimed Mrs. Berry.
"What a perfect gift! They're going to love their new home!"

But Sarah Beth had been counting. "Twenty nine!" she announced. "There's only 29."

Just then, Tyler Timothy spotted
one more ant, perfect and black,
peeking out from one of Sarah Beth's braids.
"Sarah Beth," he said.
"The thirtieth ant is on your hair."
"An ant on my hair?" Sarah Beth screamed.
"Get it off!"

So, Tyler Timothy Bradford did.

"Thirty!" he announced,
placing the ant
with all the others.

Then, bending down, he whispered so only the ants could hear,
"I'll bring you lots and lots of ooey, gooey, chocolate cupcake crumbs."

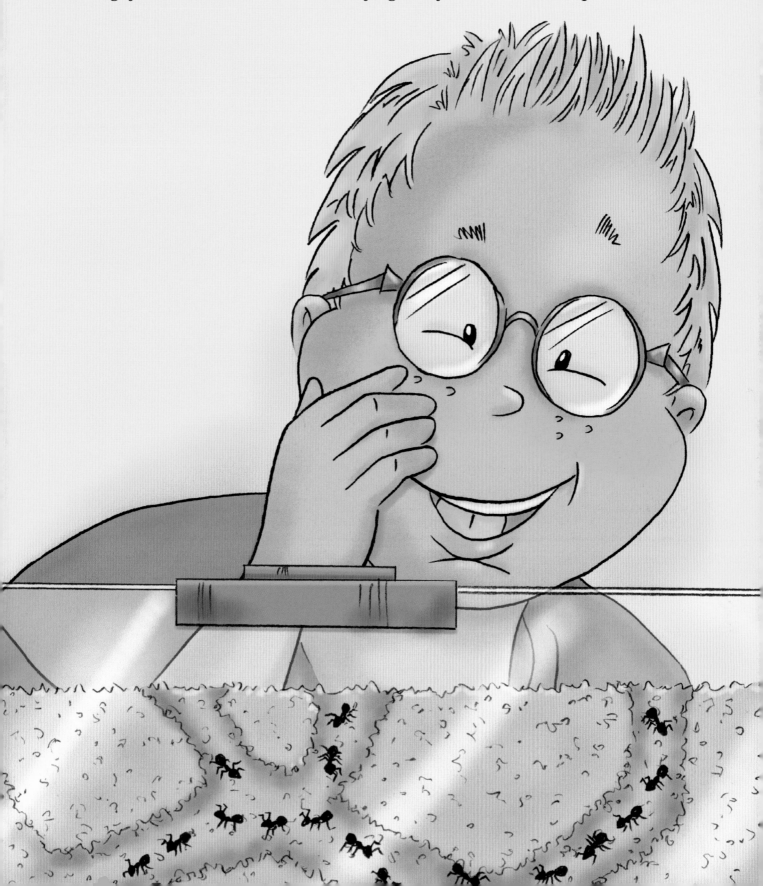

And that was something
Tyler Timothy Bradford *never* forgot.

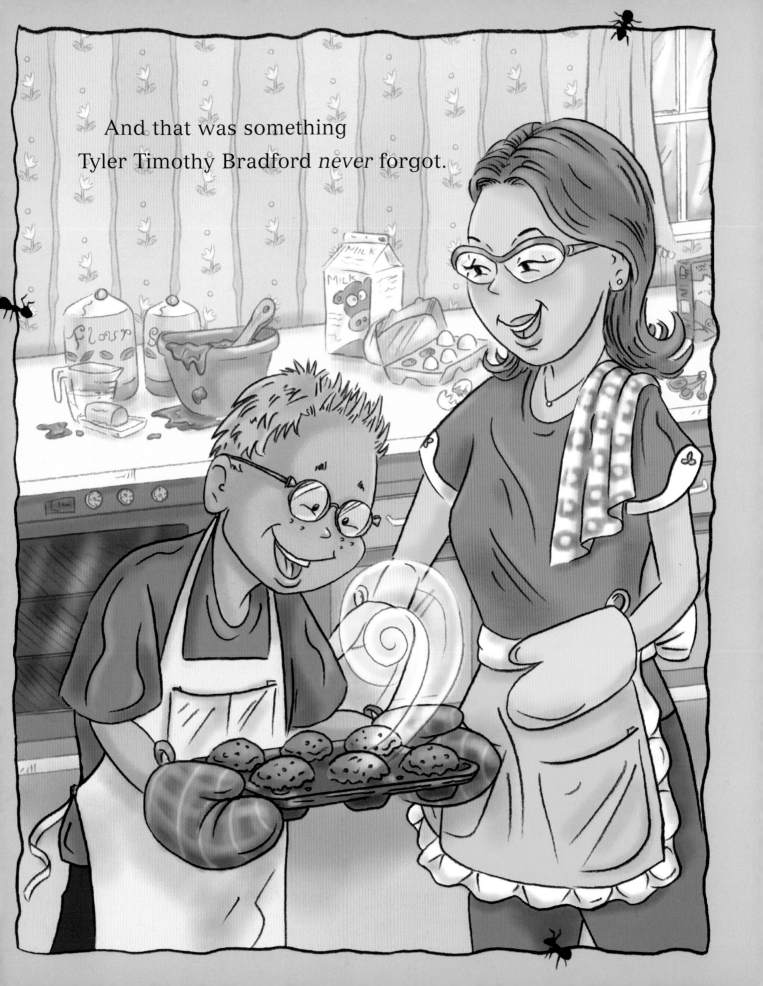